Love at

In
Ancient Egypt

Bernard Paul Badham

ISNB: 978-1-326-02451-2

http://bpbadhamauthor.com

Copyright (c) Bernard Paul Badham 2014.
All Rights Reserved.

Love and Sex in Ancient Egypt

Figure 1.
*Cleopatra depicted bare breasted and wearing the Mut cap and Hathor crown.
Hathor was the goddess of music and love.*

Introduction

The ancient Egyptians were aware of the function of the sex act and the purpose of the male semen in that act, but there were some misconceptions as to the semen's source, its route through the female body and its eventual fertilisation of the female ovum. It is this misconception about the female body, coupled with Egyptian religious belief, that will lead the reader to some surprising conclusions about ancient Egyptian temple practices.

One only has to think about the story of King Snefru's female rowers to appreciate the Egyptian's understanding of eroticism:

King Snefru having wandered around the royal palace was bored,
in search of rest and relaxation, and found none.
The Lector Priest gave him an idea,
one hopefully which would amuse and relax his master.
The priest advised him to take a boat to the palace lake
and to get the most beautiful girls of the royal harem to row for him.
Pleased with the idea Snefru called for twenty oars ebony plated with gold
and twenty beautiful virgins,
and he clothed in fish nets instead of their normal clothes.

The story records how he had them row the boat up and down the lake while he admired the banks and the nesting place for fowl!

It is evident from Egyptian literature and to a lesser extent from Egyptian art that they appreciated the pleasing and social aspects of sex and sexual relations, after all, their religious beliefs regarding the creation of the world and the origins of mankind involved a very specific sexual act.

Sex in the Creation Myth

In the creation myth according to the religious cult at Heliopolis, there was nothing at the beginning of time, but the watery waste - the primordial waters called Nun. The god Atum (in the form of the rising sun god Khepri) created a mound of earth which rose out of the waters - an act of creation which is reflected annually with the fertile black land appearing after the inundation of the Nile. Heliopolis was the site of the original creation mound.

Then Atum, 'the All', who came into being of himself began the first act of creation:

Atum copulated with himself and from his own semen life was first born.

Figure 2.
Atum is he who (once) came into being (into Kheperer the 'beetle' the young sun), who masturbated (msaw) in On. He took his phallus in his grasp that he might create orgasm by means of it, and so were born the twins Shu and Tefnut…'
Pyramid Text 527

He then gave birth to Shu (male), the god of the air and Tefnut (female) the goddess of moisture. Shu and Tefnut copulated with each other and Tefnut gave birth to Geb (male), the earth god and Nut (female) the sky goddess. It is clear from this creation account that the creator god Atum must have had both male and female attributes to his personality and physiological make-up to have given birth, of himself, to both male and female gods.

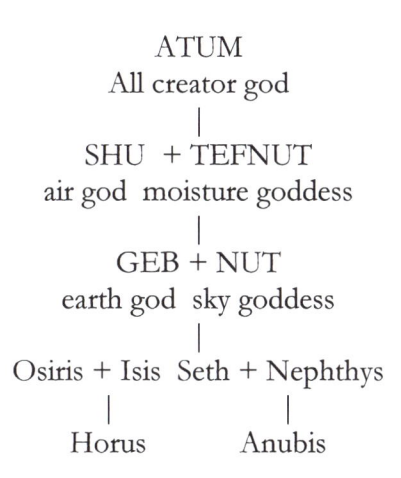

ATUM
All creator god
|
SHU + TEFNUT
air god moisture goddess
|
GEB + NUT
earth god sky goddess
|
Osiris + Isis Seth + Nephthys
| |
Horus   Anubis

It is also worth pointing out here that to produce further offspring these gods had to have brother and sister sexual relations. This may have given religious moral credence to Pharaoh marrying his own sisters - after all he was himself a god.

Figure 2.
Nut the sky goddess and Geb the Earth god copulate to produce Osiris and Isis and Seth and Nephthys

In reality the Egyptians had a simplistic and idyllic view of life and their attitudes towards sexual relations and marriage were no more complex. They would express the sexual act in simple language such as:

'The man lay with his wife one night and she became pregnant.'

We should not take this to mean they had no understanding about human physiology, for as we shall see later they had a practical knowledge of the human body - as reflected in their Medical Papyri. What is interesting is their misconceptions about the sex act and the resultant fertilisation of the female ovum. These misconceptions I believe were reflected in their religious beliefs and will allow us to draw some controversial conclusions about some of their ritual temple enactments.

Before we discuss the act specifically and these misconceptions, we will look at the Egyptian attitudes to women in general and the relationships that existed between women and men in courtship and marriage. Men and women in ancient Egypt were free to enjoy the company of each other without too many moralistic and legal ties, but we must not imagine that this encouraged promiscuity or polygamy. They had moral and communal restraints, written and unwritten, that ensured certain standards of behaviour and responsibility among married and unmarried couples, but texts referring to the subject of relationships within and without of marriage were mostly practical rather than moralistic.

Women In Ancient Egypt

The women of ancient Egypt were certainly more free and independent compared to women of other cultures in the ancient world. To be a woman in ancient Egypt was a good thing. Women of ancient Egypt were free to live exciting lives in a culture that was both romantic and exotic, they were also able to own property and enjoy the privilege of legal rights. To others in the ancient world, these were women of distinct beauty and wanton character. One only has to think of the more legendary ladies of Egyptian society, namely Nefertiti and Cleopatra to appreciate our view of Egyptian women. In Figure 2. above Nut the sky goddess arches over her husband and brother the Earth god Geb. He is ready with his erect penis to copulate with his wife and sister to produce the next generation of gods and goddesses. A papyrus shows Geb as green coloured - the colour associated with vegetation and fertility.

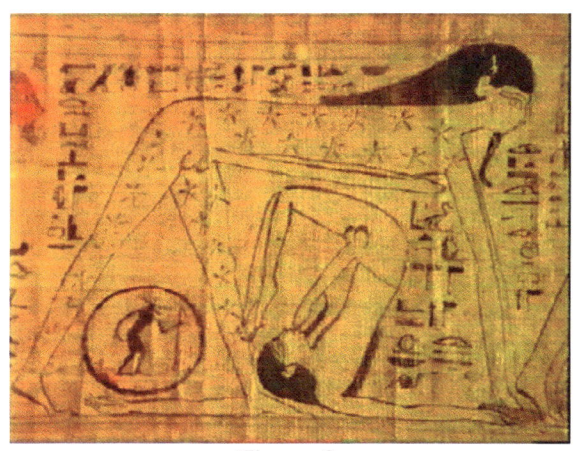

Figure 3.
This interesting image has Geb copulating with himself - swallowing his own semen. Strangely the sky goddess seems to have some male attributes, namely testicles.

Figure 4.
*Beautiful Egyptian women dressed in finely woven garments.
Each one wears a heavy wig which had erotic overtones
in the eyes of the Egyptian men.*

We have of course a slightly one-sided view of the females represented in Egyptian art. These were invariably formal paintings of Egypt's upper class: wives or daughters - women of the court, either the wives and daughters of Egyptian noble men or from the immediate family of the king. These ladies were almost always portrayed as finely dressed in the most beautiful of gowns and adorned with ornate expensive jewellery - usually made of gold and semiprecious stones such as the beautiful blue lapis-lazuli.

Their garments were made of the most finely woven linen, which made it translucent, giving a seductive image of the beautiful female body beneath.

Figure 5.
A statue of either the wife of Akhenaten or one of his daughters. It stylises the erotic way Egyptian women dressed. The garment clings to the female body accentuating the female form.

Figure 6.
Two heavy wigged females at a banquet sniff the fragrant lotus flower, itself a potent symbol for rebirth and fertility.

Very often one breast, usually the left breast, was uncovered - tantalizing the Egyptian male observer. In many cases both breasts were bare.

In tomb paintings the female was usually portrayed in a passive and supportive secondary role to her husband, who was invariably the tomb owner. Some Egyptian women did have their own tombs, the Queen Hatshepsut for instance, but usually they were buried in their husband's tomb. They were often depicted on a smaller scale compared with their male companions. This was probably a reflection of the traditional image of the man being the head of the Egyptian household.

As is typical with Egyptian art, the images of the women of ancient Egypt were stylized to show maximum detail. The single eye was viewed from the front, while the head was in profile, the torso was also shown from the front. The hips were viewed from the side and the legs were shown separate and slightly apart. This was not simplistic artistic representation, as suggested by some, but an attempt by the Egyptian artist to preserve the idealized identifying features of the individual being portrayed. The Egyptian women themselves were always depicted in youthful virile form - these were perfect physical specimens, after all this was how they were going to spend eternity in the afterlife - why have yourself portrayed as fat or ugly when the magical power of the Egyptian hieroglyphic art could keep you and transform you into an eternal beauty!

Women in the background of the main characters in a scene of typical Egyptian family life were depicted less generously. These were more natural portraits of women in Egyptian society, they were either old, poorly dressed or fat - going about their business of making bread, pulling flax in the fields or gleaning grain. It was not uncommon for the wife to be depicted with the husband by statues showing the pair seated in some kind of embrace, but this was usually quite formal, where the wife was shown in a supportive role with her arm around his shoulder or waist.

Statues of the king and queen invariably show the wife on a much smaller secondary scale. The artist almost always shows the woman in tight clinging clothes which emphasizes her sexuality by stressing the outline of her breasts. It is well known that Egyptian men took to themselves concubines - as their means could afford and as one can imagine, this did not always lead to harmony within the marriage or family group. A letter from a Middle Kingdom priest Heqanakhet to his family reads:

'He who commits any offence against my concubine, he is against me and I am against him. Look, she is my concubine and everyone knows how to treat a man's concubine.... Would any of you be patient if his wife had been denounced to him? Then why should I be patient?'

The ancient Egyptians suffered from problems in personal relationships as much as we do today. Women of ancient Egypt had access to medical treatment for a number of ailments related to 'women's matters'. The *Edwin Smith Papyrus* gives information relevant to the study of women. The treatments in the papyrus are in the form of magical texts and prescriptions for a variety of complaints. There was no clear division between amuletic magic and medicine.

Ebers Medical Papyrus.

The *Ebers Medical Papyrus* deals in part with male problems such as itching, impotence and gonorrhoea and has a long section concerned with women's matters including reproduction, contraception, breastfeeding and child welfare. Knowledge of the internal working of the female body was limited considering that the Egyptians were well studied in the process of the dissection of the deceased and subsequent mummification.

The position and importance of the uterus was known, but there is no mention of the ovaries. The uterus was believed by the ancient Egyptians to be mobile within the female body. This wandering of the uterus was harmful to the patient and treatments were developed to return it to its original position. One such treatment for a wandering uterus was fumigation with dried human excrement.

> *'Prescription to cause a woman's uterus to go to its correct place: tar that is on the wood of a ship is mixed with the dregs of excellent beer, and the patient drinks this.'*

> *There was also the assumption that a healthy woman had a free passageway connecting her womb to the rest of her body, including her digestive system.*

This is quite an important statement and as will be seen later has a direct bearing on our final conclusions regarding Egyptian religious belief and ritual.

Many fertility tests were designed to locate any obstruction in this bodily passageway to the womb which would prevent conception. One prescription requires the female patient to sit on a mixture of date flour and beer, presuming if the passage way was clear the fertile woman would vomit after treatment. The number of retches would indicate the number of potential pregnancies. One can easily imagine the potential for cheating in such a test if the woman wanted to be seen as being fertile - a great seductive and attractive attribute for an Egyptian woman.

Another test involved the use of a garlic or onion pessary which was inserted in the vagina and left overnight. If in the morning the garlic could be detected on the woman's breath she was thought to be able to receive, again this demonstrates the Egyptian's misconception about female physiology - that the digestive system was in some way connected with the womb. The Egyptian scribe Ankhsheshonq writes some words of advice concerning the treatment of wives:

> *'Let your wife see your wealth but do not trust her with it ... Do not open your heart to your wife, as what you say in private will be repeated in the street ... If a wife does not desire a husband's property, she is in love with another man.'*

The Egyptian men also thought that a 'good woman' was something to be admired and of great value:

> *'She is like food which arrives in the time of famine'*

The deviousness of some women were also recognised by Egyptian men. In the 19th Dynasty story of *'A Tale of Two Brothers'* a scheming wife of Anpu (Anubis) the elder tries to seduce his younger brother

Bata. When the attempt fails the rejected spouse falsely accuses Bata of attempted rape.

'Now the wife of his elder brother grew afraid so took fat and grease and made herself appear as if she had been beaten.'

The enraged elder brother of course wants to kill his innocent younger brother. After being warned by his favourite cow of his brother's intentions, Bata manages to escape.

The beautiful woman was certainly admired in ancient Egypt. In the story of *The Possessed Princess of Bekhten* the Prince of the country of Bekhten bringing tribute and offerings to the Pharaoh Ramesses II also offered his own daughter:

'He placed his eldest daughter at the front thereof, to show his reverence for His Majesty, and to gain favour before him. Now she was a very beautiful girl, and His Majesty thought her more beautiful than any other girl he had ever seen before, and the title of Royal Spouse, mighty lady, Ra-neferu, was straightway given to her, and when His Majesty arrived in Egypt she became in very truth the 'Royal spouse'.'

Figure 7.
Scantily dressed maidservants wait on the guests who are enjoying the banquet.

Figure 8.
A bare breasted female dancer performs - wearing only a short 'buttock skirt.'

Figure 9.
Female musicians entertain while two young girls wearing only a belt and wig dance.

Love poems describe the more intimate relations between men and women:

*'When I see your eyes shine and I press close to look at you,
most beloved of men who rules my heart.
Oh, the happiness of this hour, may it go on forever!
Since I have slept with you, you have raised up my heart.
Never leave me!'*

Love songs and romantic poems were popular throughout ancient Egypt's history. They were semi-erotic and sometimes made explicit references to sexual intercourse between lovers. They indicate that Egyptian society was relaxed in its attitude towards the relationships between two consenting adults where women could express feelings of love and sexual arousal just as much as men.

Ancient Egyptian Love Songs

The words used for 'love-songs' in the ancient Egyptian text are *tekhw* and *tekhtekhw*. It is interesting to note that the word *tekhw* also means 'to drink' and is closely related to similar hieroglyphic words, such as *tekhy* 'to become drunk' and *tekhiw* 'drunkard'. Perhaps the ancient Egyptians were reminded that one who is in love can act just as rash and as foolish as someone who is drunk. The word *tekhtekhw* also means 'to be disarranged, in wrong order, topsy-turvy, involved and confused,' all good descriptions for someone in love. The word *tekhtekhw* appears in one of the love songs in this collection: 'Her Love is a Snare'. One should note that although many of the ancient Egyptian love songs were probably put to music, they can also be regarded as love poems in their own right. In the following translations I have tried to stick to the original Egyptian words as closely as possible, leaving the poetic power of the words, their order and meaning to the original author or scribe. As you read the love songs you are as close to the original Egyptian as possible. For the wonderment of how these love songs might have sounded when spoken, I have also included the ancient Egyptian phonetic versions of the songs for the reader to sound aloud for his or her own pleasure.

The love songs known to us today come from four sources: The Chester Beatty I Papyrus, The Harris 500 Papyrus, a Turin Papyrus Fragment and a fragmentary Cairo Museum Vase.

In the following love song the scribe describes his love most intimately:

My One Love

'*My One Love, she is first in beauty among Ladies. Behold, she is like a goddess, the Wadjet Star, appearing royally in the beautiful new year, shining bright with pure white skin, and beautiful searching eyes, with sweet lips for speaking, but she is quiet. With a tall elegant neck, with breasts of lapis lazuli, and her fine straight hair, her arms and hands are an abundant gold. Her fingers are like lotus flowers. Oh, I faint at the thought of my deeply beloved's buttocks and waist, her firm thighs and her beauty, with perfect feet, she treads gently upon the ground, while she carries off my heart in her tight embrace. She makes the necks of all men turn to see her. It is pure joy to hold her tight. He is like the first of loved men. Look and behold, she comes and goes like that yonder, one and only, royal goddess.*'

'My One Love' - Commentary

'My One Love, she is first in beauty among beautiful ladies' - the Egyptian word *waty* 'one' has a strong sense of 'uniqueness' attached to it and is used by the scribe to describe his *sole* lover, who is 'not second in beauty among beautiful women'.

'Behold, she is like a goddess, the Wadjet Star' - I have used the name *Wadjet Star* to reinforce the scribe's use of 'star-goddess'. The ancient Egyptians believed the stars in the heavens to be the glorified spirits of the deceased, especially the gods and goddesses. The cobra *Wadjet* hieroglyph in the text is a determinative *glyph* for the word 'goddess'. *Wadjet* herself was the goddess of the North ie Upper Egypt.

'Appearing royally in the beautiful new year' - the annual inundation was heralded by the helical rising of the star Sirius and was therefore, the beginning of the Egyptian calendar New Year. The appearance of the star and the inundation was a time for celebration and joy. The inundation meant that Egypt would once again be able to sow seed and reap a harvest to feed its hungry population.

'Shining bright with pure white skin' - in Egyptian art the men were portrayed with sun-tanned skin, whereas the women with white skin, a sign of affluence and dignity, since they had not worked outdoors like the common folk.

'And beautiful searching eyes' - the word *gmhew* means 'look, to espy'. His lover's eyes he sees as piercing and beautiful.

'With sweet lips for speaking' the glyph in the word for sweet, was probably a sweet tasting root.

'But she is quiet' - ancient Egyptian texts record that 'the man speaks, but the woman is quiet', quietness in a woman being regarded as a virtue.

'With a tall elegant neck' - one is reminded of the bust of the beautiful Nefertiti, chief wife of Khenaten. The bust is an elegant portrait of a very beautiful woman with a long sensuous neck, perhaps an erotic attribute for women in the eyes of Egyptian men.

'With breasts of lapis lazuli' - Egyptians regarded the deep blue colour of the precious mineral to imitate the heavens. Lapis lazuli was almost as precious to the ancient Egyptians as gold or silver. It was used in jewellery and was the colour of the god Amun - it was the 'skin of the gods'. Egyptian women would paint their breasts gold and their nipples lapis lazuli blue to entice their lovers. The word 'true' in the texts could refer to the *true* lapis lazuli, rather than the lighter blue clay faience.

'And her fine straight hair' - the word for 'true' in Egyptian is *maat*, synonymous with the goddess of 'truth, order and justice' and in an abstract form means 'straight'. Maat's 'feather of truth' appears as a glyph in text.

'Her arms are an abundant gold' - gold 'the immortal and imperishable flesh of the gods' and could also be a reference to the gold arm bands, bracelets and rings worn by rich Egyptian women.

'Her fingers are like lotus flowers' - lotus flowers were the symbol of rebirth and regeneration for the afterlife. The sun-god Ra appeared on an emerging lotus flower out of the primeval waters of chaos to give life and light to the world. The lotus flower was also the symbol of the South, Upper Egypt and had erotic connotations. The lotus flower was used at Egyptian banquets, where the lotus was presented to the nose for the perfume. The leaves of the lotus were also crushed and mixed with wine as an aphrodisiac, hence 'fingers like lotus flowers'. Recent scientific studies have shown that the blue lotus, *Nymphaea caerulea,* if ingested has the same chemical and physiological effects as modern Viagra, hence its erotic connotations in Egyptian art and love poetry.

'Oh I faint at the sight of my deeply beloved's buttocks and waist, her firm thighs and her beauty' - The scribe describes with emotion the longing for his lover's female form.

We assume he is speaking of the perfectness of form of his beloved's buttocks, rather than size.

'With perfect feet, she treads gently upon the ground' - beautiful Egyptian women portrayed in the images of tombs and temples were usually bare foot. The feet shown bare, as was the neck and breast, were the erotic parts of a woman's body. The scribe describes her as one who is light foot, suggesting slimness and elegance.

'While she carries off my heart in her tight embrace' - her loving embrace causes him to surrender his heart to his lover.

'She makes the necks of all men turn to see her' - her stunning beauty is such that *all men turn* and take a *second look* as she walks by.

'It is pure joy to hold her tight' - this wonderfully describes the delight his lover gives him, *it is all joy* to hold her and to hold her tight.

'Like the first of loved men' - he describes himself as the first man to truly love and to *be* truly loved.

'Look and behold, she comes and goes' - he is excited at her coming and going, he watches her every move.

'Like that yonder, one and only, royal goddess' - he finishes by reminding us of his first thoughts about her, that she is his *one and only* and compares her to the Star Goddess.

We must not let this apparent sexual freedom confuse us into thinking 'everything goes' in ancient Egypt. Sleeping with another man's wife was frowned upon, equally 'going off' with a loose seductive temptress was something that was warned against. Homosexuality was certainly not condoned. In the *Chapter of the Negative Confession* in the 'Book of the Dead,' the deceased confesses the things that he did *not do* in life including 'copulating with young boys.'

The husband was the head of the Egyptian household, while the wife, helped by her unmarried daughters, ran the house as a daily routine. In the eyes of the law, man and wife were equal. The Egyptian woman had the right to inherit and buy and sell property.

> *'I am a free woman of Egypt. I have raised eight children, and have provided them with everything suitable to their station in life. But now I have grown old and behold, my children don't look after me anymore. I will therefore give my goods to the ones who have taken care of me. I will not give anything to the ones who have neglected me.' Last will and testament of the Lady Naunakhte.*

The property acquired by a couple during marriage was joint owned by husband and wife and therefore this was an addition to that which she already owned. A share of this joint possession, was passed on to her children at her death or to the woman herself if she was divorced.

The Greek historian Herodotus records that only Egyptian priests were expected to remain monogamous, this implies that polygamy was common. Marriage of an Egyptian man to more than one wife would have been restricted to the more affluent - a rich man's privilege.

Some more advice concerning Egyptian women:

> *'Do not take to yourself a woman whose husband is still alive, in case he should become your enemy!'* Scribe Ankhsheshonq

A woman's love for a man she could not possess can be felt in the following verse:

> *'He is my neighbour who lives near my mother's house, but I cannot go to him. Mother is right to tell him 'stop seeing her'. It pains my heart to think of him, and I am possessed of my love for him. Truly he is foolish, but I am just the same. He does not know how much I long to embrace him, or he would send word to my mother.'*
> New Kingdom love poem

A New Kingdom love song gives us some idea of the love expressed by an Egyptian woman:

> *'I shall not leave him even if they beat me and I have to spend the day in the swamp. Not even if they chase me to Syria with clubs, or to Nubia with palm ribs, or even into the desert with sticks or to the coast with reeds. I will not listen to their plans for me to give up the man I love.*

Advice for choosing a husband:

> *'Choose a prudent husband, not necessarily a rich one, for your daughter.'*

It was usually the father that chose a husband for his daughter.

There were no legal age restriction on marriage, partners were ready for marriage at the onset of puberty and sometimes even before. 'Teenagers' were rare in ancient Egypt for as soon as they were able, sons and daughters were married off to suitable partners. One can understand why Egyptian 'men and women' married so young, considering the average life span for a man was some 33 years while that for a woman was a few years less. On average men lived longer than women simply because of the complications which could arise during childbirth.

For a young Egyptian girl the onset of puberty and menstruation would have occurred at about the age of 14. It is reasonable to assume that marriage for young girls in Ancient Egypt occurred between the ages of 11 to 14 assuming there was a suitable partner available and that the father had approved of the arrangement. During the Graeco-Roman Period of Egyptian history there is evidence of young girls marrying at the tender age of eight or nine.

An unmarried daughter past this age, would have simply remained with the mother. She would face a life of domesticity, helping to run the Egyptian household. The household would have been made up of husband and chief wife, plus two or three mistresses and if the man was sufficiently affluent, his sons and remaining unmarried daughters and his widowed mother and usually his married daughters and their husbands. As the family unit grew structural additions could be made to the house. Slaves, both men and women would be accommodated for. In the case of young female slaves the husband had the right and access to sexual relations with them.

The age recommended for men to marry was twenty years or at least he should wait until he became a 'respectable man'. Inevitably the man was older and more mature than his younger bride. It is probable that young brides were sexually active before the onset of menstruation and that young mothers must have contributed to infant and maternal mortality. A young and beautiful Egyptian girl dedicated to the service of Amun gives us some indication of the widespread acceptance of pre-pubertal sex:

> *'She becomes a prostitute and has intercourse with whoever she likes until the purification of her body takes place.' Strabo*

The purification mentioned is the onset of menstruation, this indicates that this young girl was encouraged to have sex before the age of puberty. Marriage was normal between first cousins, but there are various accounts of brother and sister being married - the sister more than likely being a half sister.

> *'I see my sister coming. My heart exults and my arms open to embrace her.
> My heart pounds in its place just as the red fish leaps in its pond.
> Oh night, be mine forever, now that my lover has come.' New Kingdom love song*

There was no legal or religious marriage ceremony, but one can imagine the actual occasion of a father 'giving his daughter away' would have been one in which the Egyptians would love to celebrate - the celebrations lasting several days. The young bride physically leaving her father's home and entering her husband's to consummate the marriage would have been act enough. Her allegiance was also transferred from father to husband. She took with her the 'goods of a woman', her possessions and property.

Defloration of the young bride, even up until recent times, included the groom or a female relation placing a finger wrapped in a clean cloth into the vagina and breaking the hymen. The show of blood being necessary to prove her purity. In some cases to prove the purity of the young bride and to show that she was without child, there would be a long isolation period of some six months where the young girl was not to come near any man.

At the time of the wedding ceremony the father of the bride would hand over a considerable amount of goods, mostly grain to keep the young couple going for a few years - at least until they were established as a respectable couple. Although there were no legal documents signed at the time of marriage, very often the couple would draw up a type of marriage contract which would decide how the joint wealth would be split up in the event of death or divorce.

'If I divorce you as my wife, and hate you, preferring to take another woman as my wife, I will give you two pieces of silver besides the two pieces of silver I have given you as your woman's portion ... And I will give you one third of everything which will be owned by you and myself furthermore.' Horemheb. Graeco-Roman contract.

The majority of marriages ended by the couple simply splitting up. The wife left the matrimonial home and returned with her possessions and her share of the joint property to her family home.

'Do not divorce a woman of your household if she does not conceive and does not give birth'. Late Period scribal advice

From the Middle Kingdom onwards, at least, it was the right of an Egyptian man to end an 'unhappy' marriage - if there was no good reason for him divorcing his wife or if he had done it unfairly he would have to pay a fine to the wife's family. There is documented evidence that a wife could divorce her husband from the New Kingdom onwards.

Women caught in the act of adultery risked the repudiation of the community and loss of legal rights. It was 'the great sin which is found in women' and was the most serious marital crime and certainly a reason for divorce. In cases of adultery the woman was seen as the temptress while the man was seen as the innocent partner. Egyptian texts are full of warnings for men to stay clear of other men's wives who would use their feminine wiles to snare them into sexual relationships:

'Then she spoke to him, saying, 'You are very strong. I see your vigour every day.' And she desired to know him as a man. She got up, took hold of him and said 'Come let us spend an hour lying in bed together. It will be good for you, and afterwards I will make you some fine new clothes.'
New Kingdom Tale of Two Brothers

In the following love song the man describes his lover 'as a snare:'

Her Love is a Snare

'Love Songs bear witness to the truth of the provision of my sister. With her skilful hands like lotus buds and her breast of ripe berries, her arm is twined like vine stems (around me). Her face is a snare of fine precious wood (to trap me). I am like the goose (who is caught), so then, as to these my fledglings (children), which are as a bait of worms to snare a catch of fish, she gives (them) to me.'

Commentary

'Love Songs bear witness to the truth' – the poem used the word *tekhtekhw* 'love songs'. He suggests that songs written, or perhaps other songs, that he has himself has was written about her tell of the beauty of his love.

'Of the provision of my sister' – he is in wonderment of the beauty and nature of his lover. He proceeds to describe her.

'With skilful hands like lotus buds' – he likens the touch of her hands to the beautiful soft and erotic lotus flower.

'And her breasts of ripe berries' – her breasts are soft, round, firm and good 'to eat'?

'Her arm is twined like vine stems (around me)' – the description of his love takes on a dualistic note. Her arms around him is desirable, but perhaps he feels slightly trapped by her embrace.

'Her face is a snare of fine precious wood' – good wood was expensive in ancient Egypt, cedar for instance was imported from Lebanon. The beauty of her face attracted him, snared him. He is captivated by her looks.

'I am like the goose' – the goose was caught, trapped in a net, for the killing.

'Then as to these my fledglings' – possibly the children which she has born him.

'Which are as a bait of worms to snare a catch of fish' – he feels perhaps their offspring were a ploy to trap him.

'She gives them to me' – it is as though he was unaware of their existence and now she comes to him, perhaps using them in a proposal of marriage.

Men were certainly warned repeatedly to guard against the loose woman, the pretty young girl who would entrap him with her wiles - her character was devious and her ways, looks and advances were a snare to him, for after all had not even the goddess Isis schemed and obtained the secret name of the god Ra by making a poisonous snake out of his own spittle?

Incompatibility and infertility of the woman were usual reasons for divorce, though in some cases where the wife was unable to bear children the husband might resort to a secondary wife or concubine and hence 'save' the marriage. A 21st Dynasty letter from the workman's village at Deir el Medina describes how a man, having fallen in love with another woman, divorces his wife after twenty years of marriage with the feeble excuse:

'I repudiate you because you have no sight in one eye'.

The wife rebukes him for having taken so long to notice.

An Old kingdom story read to king Khufu by his son Khafre relates the affairs of the wife of a lector priest. It was told to Khufu in order to amuse him while he watched the building of the Great Pyramid. The wife of the Lector Priest of King Djoser was in love with a certain townsman. The townsman said to the wife:

'Let us go and enjoy ourselves in the pavilion by the gate.'

This was in the Lector Priest's own garden. So they went and enjoyed themselves passing the day in drinking. The townsman went for an evening swim in the Priest's lake. The whole affair was observed by the house steward and was reported to her husband Ebaoner who was also a magician. The priest made a life-size wax model of a crocodile and put a spell over it:

'Whoever comes to bathe in my lake do you seize him and hold him.'

The priest told the steward to throw the wax model into the lake when the townsman went to bathe. The next time the priest went away, the wife and the townsman met in the lake pavilion, while the steward watched on. When the man went for his evening swim the steward threw in the wax crocodile and it came alive and grabbed the man in its jaws and took him to the bottom of the lake. The priest returned seven days later with King Djoser and called the crocodile to the surface with the townsman still in its jaws. The priest asked the King to make judgement on the pair of lovers. The king decided that the crocodile should take away that which was his, the man and had the woman taken to a field north of the Royal Residence and had her burnt alive and her ashes scattered in the Nile.

This story probably contained an element of truth concerning the two lovers and was therefore told as a warning to any wife who may have a lustful eye and to those men who would dare sleep with another man's wife.

> *'Man is more anxious to copulate than a donkey.*
> *What restrains him is his purse.'*
> Observations of the scribe Ankhsheshonq

It has been mentioned that infidelity and infertility were grounds for divorce in ancient Egypt. Divorce was not uncommon where a couple who had been living together would simply separate. From about 500 BC onwards women could initiate divorce probably on the grounds of infidelity. In cases of infertility the woman was always to blame as male infertility was probably not understood. Other reasons for a man wanting to divorce his wife, was 'the dislike of one's wife' or simply the 'wish to marry another'. The latter reason for divorce was linked to a young man's aspiring career. As he rose up through the offices of the bureaucratic ladder he aspired to marry women of high standing and greater influence. One man in a letter to his dead wife reminds her of how he married her when he was young and how he stayed with her and 'did not cause her to grieve' or 'divorce her' as he was 'carrying out all sorts of offices for the Pharaoh.'

One reason for a man to re-marry was of course the death of his wife. This may have been common when one considers the dangers associated with child birth. Some women are referred to as 'former wives' in the tombs of men, whether these women were separated from their husband through divorce or death is unclear.

The Workmen's Village at Deir el Medina
The workman's village at Deir el Medina housed the workmen who were working in the Valley of the Kings during the New Kingdom Period. The village not only housed the craftsmen who were working on the tombs of the Kings of Egypt, but also their families.

It is probable that marriage to more than one woman at the same time was restricted to the more elite members of Egyptian society and that polygamy was simply a matter of affluence. The everyday Egyptian man may not have been able to afford more than one wife. In any case, the men of ancient Egypt would have had sexual access to any female in his household who was a servant, slave or woman of lower social standing. It would have only been the head of the household who would have had sexual relations with the female servants. A son records specifically how he did not have sexual relations with his father's servants. The man would have had children by these secondary wives, concubines or servant girls, which would have formed part of the household but would probably not have the same rights as those children born by his 'first wife.'

Ostraca, scribbled writings on broken bits of pottery, found at the site give record the daily messages sent between households and offices. One woman at Deir el Medina conceived a child by one man while she was the *hemet* 'wife, woman' of another. A court statement from a text at this site declares:

> '*A wife (hemet) is (a) wife. She should not make love.*
> *She should not have sexual intercourse.*'

It is clear that this refers to the wife's sexual relations other than her husband meaning a woman should be sexually faithful to her man. One of the probable reasons for this degree of fidelity on the part of the woman was:

It was easy to determine who one's mother was, but not who was one's father!'

Hmt *hemet* 'woman, wife'

To be sure that the children born of his wife were his own and not another man's, a husband had to ensure faithfulness on the part of his wife, after all, he wouldn't want a child to inherit his wealth other than his own. Maternity, unlike paternity was never in doubt. When it came to describing the man's offspring, the child was described as being:

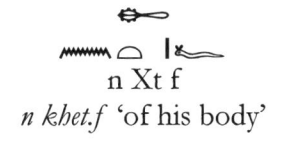

n Xt f
n khet.f 'of his body'

With regards to the mother, the child was described as being:

mswt n
meswt n 'born of'

This distinction may have been related to the fact that the father provided the seed (sperm) while the mother, who allowed this seed to grow in the fertile 'soil' of her womb, with the aid of the gods, conceived the child.

Children inherited property from their mother as well as their father. It is not surprising then, that adultery on the part of the wife was deplored and that men were criticised in the texts for having affairs with married women.

Young men scribes were often warned about having sexual relations with prostitutes, not because of the moral aspects of the encounters, but simply because it distracted from their studies. It appears that sexual relations with women, other than married women, was an accepted part of Egyptian social life. It was okay for a man to have sexual relations with his servants, concubines or secondary wives as long as he did not interfere with another man's wife or women of his household.

A legal case in the workman's village of Deir el Medina opens with the accusation:

'You copulated with a married woman in 'the place of carrying torches''

Another case refers to the rather copious sexual activities of Paneb, a chief worker at Deir el Medina. Apart from other complaints about his rather dubious character, he was accused of having sex with a number of the workmen's wives:

*Paneb ('the lord') had intercourse with the citizeness Tuy,
when she was the wife of the workman Qenna.
He had intercourse with the citizeness Hunero,
when she was with Pendua.*

> *He had intercourse with the citizeness Hunero,*
> *when she was with Hesyunebef....*
> *When he had intercourse with Hunero,*
> *he had intercourse with Webkhet, her daughter.*
> *And Aapehty ('Great Strength'), his son,*
> *had intercourse with Webkhet as well.'*

It is not known whether the women mentioned above had sexual intercourse with Paneb of their own free will or whether they were forced. It may have been that Paneb was abusing his position of authority and that these women reluctantly had sex with him, perhaps fearing that their husbands might have lost their jobs.

The disapproval of men having sex with married women is reflected in the previously mentioned Book of the Dead. In the 'Negative Confession the deceased declares:

> *'I have not copulated with a married woman.'*

Another text warns other men of the dangers of becoming involved with certain women:

> *'Beware of a woman who is a stranger,*
> *One not known in her town;*
> *Don't stare at her when she goes by,*
> *Do not know her carnally,*
> *A deep water whose course is unknown,*
> *Such is a woman away from her husband.*
> *'I am pretty' she tells you daily,*
> *When she has no witnesses;*
> *She is ready to ensnare you,*
> *A great deadly crime when it is heard.'*
> *Instructions of Any.*
> *New Kingdom Period.*

The woman referred to in the text is obviously a married woman, away from her husband and on the lookout for an affair. This woman is trouble the author warns.

Other advice about approaching women:

> *'If you want to make friendship last in a house you enter,*
> *whether as lord, or brother, or friend,*
> *in any place you enter,*
> *beware of approaching women!*
> *The place where this is done cannot be good;*
> *there can be no cleverness in revealing this.*
> *A thousand men are turned away from their good:*
> *a little moment, the likeness of a dream,*
> *and death is reached by knowing them.*
> *It is a vile thing, conceived by an enemy;*
> *one emerges from doing it*
> *with a heart rejecting it.*
> *As for him who ails through lusting after them (the women),*
> *no plan of his can ever succeed.'*
> *Instructions of Ptah-hotep.*
> *Middle Kingdom Period.*

Again at Deir el-Medina a man was caught in bed with another workman's wife. Even though there were complaints made against him he managed to make the woman pregnant. This man was of a higher social standing than the woman's husband who was the one who was punished by a beating for having said such a thing. In another case at Deir el-Medina a married man after having an eight month affair with another woman has managed to stir up the local community who are threatening to go and beat up the woman and her household:

> *'eight full months until today he is sleeping with that woman,*
> *though he is not the husband...*
> *if he were the husband,*
> *would he then not have sworn his oath concerning your woman.'*

It appears from the text that the man has taken up with another woman without having divorced his wife. A steward stops the angry crowd and giving the advice that if the man wants to stay with this other woman he must first divorce his wife thus allowing her to remarry.

Marriage and bringing up children was accepted as a good thing in ancient Egypt. A young man was advised to take a wife while he was still young and that 'she should bear for you while you are youthful,' and 'she is a fertile field for her lord.' This idea of the woman's womb being the fertile ground for the sowing of the man's seed is repeated and strengthens the notion that a woman's attractiveness was in her ability to bear children.

Concubines

It was custom in ancient Egypt for a man whether married or unmarried to have concubines (*hbswt*) - an official mistress. These ladies who satisfied, presumably, the sexual needs of their owners had none of the legal rights accorded to married women. These 'mistresses of the house' were more than likely maids or servants in the household and indeed sometimes they were slaves given to the man as a reward for services rendered to the king during battle. Although there was a kind of sexual freedom, men still had to take care when it came to taking a sexual partner:

> *'Do not fornicate with a married woman.*
> *He who fornicates with a married woman on her bed,*
> *his wife will be copulated with on the ground.'*
> *Late Period advice to young men.*

Apparently there was no Egyptian word for bride. Terms used for married women were *hemet* 'wife, woman' and *henut* 'mistress'.

Hnt
henut
'mistress'

Egyptians displayed no false prudery when it came to the subject of sex. Potency and fertility were important attributes and were needed for enjoyment in this life and the next, in the Afterlife. False penises were moulded on to the mummified bodies of men and false nipples were attached to the mummies of women. These would serve them in the afterlife, where they would become fully functional. There was no distinction in the Egyptian mind between sexual enjoyment and the wish to produce children. A woman's fertility contributed to her sexual attractiveness. While love songs, poems and stories make vague reference to sexual intercourse, graffiti on walls and potsherds are explicit and more basic.

The Turin Erotic Papyrus

The *Turin Erotic Papyrus* is one of the earliest examples of pornography and contains a series of drawings depicting athletic couples in a number of wide ranging and difficult looking poses:

Figure 10.
A prostitute wearing a wig and belt allows entry by a middle aged Egyptian man who has an enlarged erect penis.

The Turin Erotic Papyrus was probably circulated amongst the military of Egyptian society. It contains a number of scenes (12 episodes) showing the erotic adventures of a middle aged man with a young prostitute. Captions give details of their conversation:

'Let me make it nice for you.'
'Do not be afraid.'
'You're with me, look!'
'O you naughty man!'

The young woman is scantily clad with only a wig, necklace, arm bangles, earrings and a belt girdle. The size of the man's penis is exaggerated and although he appears to be circumcised he was probably not a priest.

Figure 11.
The active couple try out various positions including the use of a chariot and entry from behind

Egyptian priests shaved their whole body, but the man depicted is balding and has facial hair. After intercourse the young woman can be seen tidying herself up ready for the next sexual encounter. In the text the woman is referred to as being of the profession *heset*, which means that she was a singing girl in the service of Hathor, goddess of love. From ostraca it would seem that the more favourable position for intercourse was 'face to face' and 'from behind'.

There is a graffiti showing Senenmut entering Hatshepsut from behind

Herodotus. who was fascinated by the unusual aspects of Egyptian life records that:

'In my lifetime a monstrous thing happened in this province, a woman having open intercourse with a he-goat.'

Necrophilia, the abuse of fresh dead female bodies in the embalming house, was also hinted at by Herodotus. The aim of normal sexual relations between a husband and wife was to produce a large family. Children were regarded as a blessing in ancient Egypt. One 11th Dynasty army captain boasted about having fathered 'seventy children, the issue of one wife.' If this boast was true one can only feel sorry for his wife.

Certain vegetables were strongly equated with fertility. The Egyptian lettuce grew tall and straight and when pressed it emitted a milky-white liquid. It is not surprising then that this vegetable became associated with the ithyphallic god of vegetation and procreation, Min.

The *cos* lettuce was highly recommended by the medical papyri as a sure cure for male impotence. It was also regarded as an aphrodisiac. The god Min was worshipped in earlier times as a fetish, rather like a barbed arrow. This has been interpreted as the union of man and woman. The god Min, as the god of fertility, was represented in human form with his legs placed tight together like those of a mummy. He had an erect phallus and a flail above his erect hand. Upon his head was a cap of two plumes and he had two streamers hanging down his back.

The hieroglyphs above Min's head give his name as

Amen-Ra, King of the gods, Lord of Heaven.

This inscription gives us the identity of the god Min - the ithyphallic representation of the god Amen who was worshipped at Karnak. As I said before, the ancient Egyptians were aware of the function of the sex act and the purpose of the male semen in that act, but there were some *misconceptions* as to the semen's source and to its route through the female body and its eventual fertilisation of the female ovum.

The Pharaoh's divine origins are well described: Some god or other, in the 18th Dynasty it was Amun, took on the guise of the present Queen's husband and entered her bedroom and made love to her. The most familiar account of divine birth is that of Hatshepsut's. The god of Thebes, Amun, is advised about the Queen-mother designate by the wise god Thoth:

> 'The girl you spoke of is called Ahmose.
> She is fairer than any woman in this land.
> She is the wife of the ruler Ankhkheperkara (Tuthmosis I),
> King of Upper and Lower Egypt,
> who is endowed with life everlasting ...'

Amun disguises himself as King Tuthmosis and is led into Queen Ahmose's presence by the god Thoth:

> 'The sublime Amun,
> Lord of the throne of the Two Lands
> had transformed himself into His Majesty her husband,
> King of Upper and Lower Egypt.
> He found her asleep amid the luxury of her palace.
> Awakened by the divine fragrance,
> she smiled upon His Majesty.
> He thereupon approached her ardently
> and showed himself in his god-like form.
> She rejoiced at the sight of his beauty.
> His love suffused her whole body
> and the palace was filled with the divine sweetness
> of all the perfumes of the land of Punt.'

This account is inscribed upon the walls of her temple at Deir el-Bahari. The next scene shows the couple conversing:

> 'After he had done with her all that he would,
> Ahmose the Royal Consort and Mother (of Hatshepsut)
> said to his Majesty,
> the sublime god Amun:
> 'How mighty is your strength, my lord!
> Your countenance, how magnificent!
> You have united my majesty with your own glory.
> My whole body is imbued with you.'
> Then Amun, Lord of the throne of the Two Lands,
> said to her: 'Khenemetamun Hatshepsut is the name of your <u>son</u>,
> whom I have placed within your body ..."

It is interesting to note that Hatshepsut describes herself as a son in an effort to legitimise herself as an heir to the throne. Another interesting thing is that the god had to disguise himself as the Queen's husband before he could make advances towards her. One wonders if this act was indeed carried out, where, perhaps on their first night of marriage, the husband did in fact dress up and come in the guise of a god to his new wife. The Egyptians had 4 words for the act of copulation: *da, nehep, rekh and nekh*. One wonders if the latter, *nekh*, has anything to do with the modern expression: *nekking*.

Familiarity with the idea of insemination is apparent in other legends and is hinted at in depictions of the god Min in the act of ejaculation from an erect penis. For the sexual organ the Egyptians used the word *henen* and funnily enough the term used for the testicles *kherwy* 'the two which are under'. The hieroglyph depicting the male phallus was used in many words concerning the idea of masculinity, but was not restricted to that use. Medical papyri reveal some of the Egyptians misconceptions - the Ebers papyrus describes how the two vesicles leading into the testicles conducts the sperm from its supposed source: the bones. This notion may be related to the Egyptian belief that a child acquires all its hard tissue from its father and the soft ones from its mother.

The anatomy of the female reproductive system were only broadly understood. Documents speak of the uterus, the *shed* and the vagina as the *septy shed*, septy meaning lips. Interestingly, the womb (and in some cases the placenta) is referred to as the *mwt remtj*, 'the mother of mankind.'

The name *wenw* applied to the developing foetus. There is no evidence that the Egyptians had any knowledge of the female contribution to fertilisation, namely the ova or eggs of the ovary. It was probably thought that the womb was simply a place for the development of the *wenw*. This seems strange for a society which was matriarchal. The Egyptians placed great importance on motherhood. The son and heir to the throne would still have to marry a daughter of royal descent to inherit the throne - this normally being the eldest daughter of the Queen

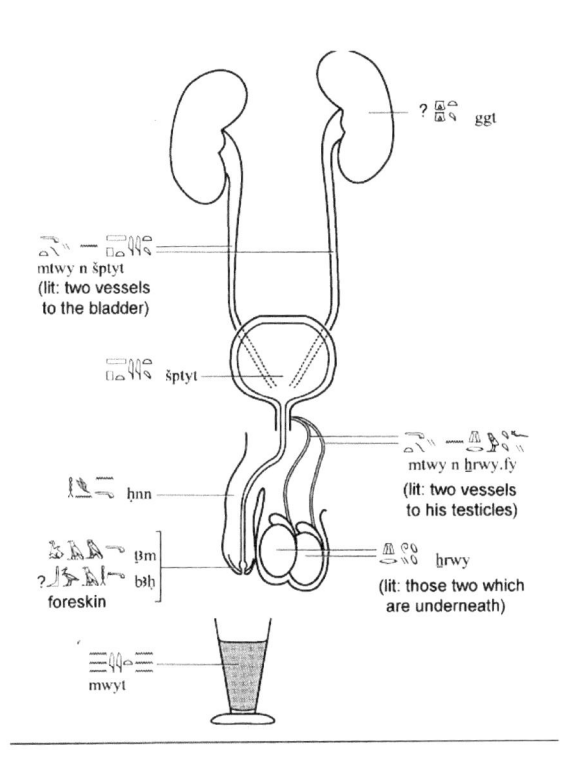

Figure 12.
The ancient Egyptian names of the male reproductive parts.

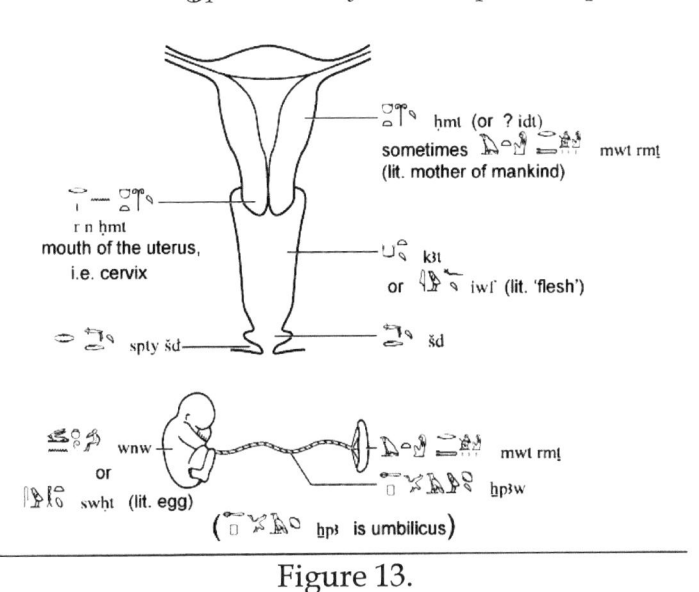

Figure 13.
The ancient Egyptian names of the female reproductive parts.

The ancient Egyptians falsely believed that the reproductive system and the digestive system were linked. This imaginary connection had its cosmological parallel in the story of the sky-goddess Nut swallowing the sun each evening and giving birth to it again each morning, likewise she ate up the stars at daybreak and released them from her womb at night.

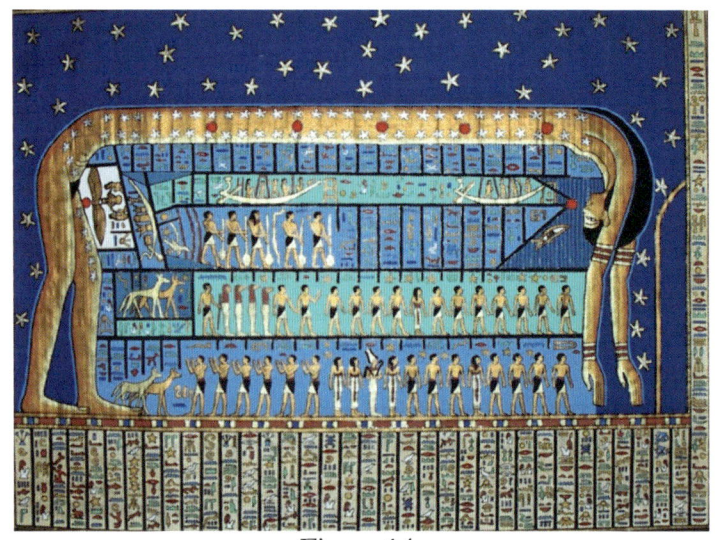

Figure 14.
Nut the sky goddess at sunset swallows the sun through her mouth and gives birth to it each morning through her vagina.

Figure 15.
Nut the sky goddess as represented by the arched Milky Way.

The idea that the reproductive and digestive systems were connected may have been inspired by the rare cases of extra-uterine pregnancy, this is when the embryo emerges from the throat or rectum. This also gave rise to the notion among the Egyptians that non-genital intercourse (oral sex) could lead to conception. The ideas of non-genital intercourse appears in Egyptian stories (The Tale of Two Brothers) and creation myths.

> *'His Majesty caused skilful workmen to go and cut down Pharaoh's trees, and as the Royal Spouse, the sacred lady herself stood looking on, a splinter flew off and went into the sacred lady's mouth, and she swallowed it and conceived.'*
> Tale of the Two Brothers XVIII

From this account it is clear the Egyptians thought that when the semen entered through the woman's mouth it had direct access to the womb, where the seed could germinate:

> *'Who makes seed grow in women and creates people from sperm. Who feeds the son in his mother's womb and soothes him to still his tears. Nurse in the womb. Giver of breath. To nourish all that he has made.'*
> The Great Hymn to the Aten

Here the god Aten is the one which causes the man's seed to grow in the woman's womb. This highlights the Egyptian belief that the sperm was the seed which grew in the womb and that they were not aware of the women's contribution to the process of fertilisation, namely the provision of the egg from the ovaries. Since the man could visibly produce the seed for fertilisation, it is likely that infertility was the fault of the woman. After all, seed planted in fertile soil would surely germinate - since the seed did not grow it must be the woman's womb which is infertile, hence the link between fertility and the god of fertility and vegetation, the god Min.

> *The god Atum, in the beginning of creation to procreate the other gods, swallowed his own seed.*

Atum was the creator god of Heliopolis. It was 'He who came into being of himself,' before heaven and earth were separated he was the 'Lord of All.'

In the Pyramid Texts he appears as the Primeval Hill:

> *'Stand upon it, this earth which issued from Atum, ...'*
> Pyramid Texts 199

The Temple of Karnak

It was at the temple of Karnak in southern power capital of ancient Egypt that the annual festival of Opet began. Every morning before dawn the priests carried out the ceremony of the re-enactment of the original (sexual) act of creation, when Atum masturbated, copulated with himself to bring into being the first gods and bring order (out of chaos) to the universe. Once a year this initial act of creation was carried out by the God, Pharaoh, and his wife, appropriately called the God's Hand. These enactments ensure, that daily, and annually, the sun rose, the inundation came and the universe remained in order. The Egyptians feared that without these ceremonies performed by the god, Pharaoh himself, or the priests standing in his place, it would fall back into chaos.

Figure 16.
The pharaoh Senwasret I before the ithyphallic god Min (Amun-Ra)

Atum begat by copulating with himself:

'Atum is he who once came into being, who masturbated in On (Heliopolis).

> *He took his phallus in his grasp that he might*
> *create orgasm by means of it,*
> *and so were born the twins Shu and Tefnut'*
> Pyramid Texts 1294

This belief in non-genital procreation, was possibly tied up with one of the rituals carried out at the Temple of Karnak, where it is believed that the creation myth was re-enacted during a secret ceremony, once a year, between the God-Pharaoh and his Great Royal Wife.

Women and Temple Ritual

Women were employed in the temples in a number of ways. A very respectable position for a woman involved with temple ritual was *Shemayt* 'Chantress, singer.'

In general, women attached to the temple were called *Heyst* 'Favoured Ones, female singer'. This was the same term used to describe concubines. 'Favoured Ones' could marry and have many children. The woman in charge of the Favoured Ones was called the *Matron of the God's Harem*.

Tuya, the mother of Tiy and grandmother of Akhenaten, had this title in the cult of the fertility god Min at Akhmin. Another title for women attached to the temple was *Duat Netjer* 'Divine Adoratrice.' This title occurred in the 18th Dynasty and by the Third Intermediate Period it became associated with the title *God's Wife of Amun*.

The title *God's Wife of Amun* was used in the 18th Dynasty and was a title conferred upon the ancestral mother of the Queens of Egypt during this period Ahmose-Nefertari. Ahmose-Nefertari was the wife of Ahmose the founder of the 18th Dynasty. This honoured title was handed down from heir to heir, mother to daughter. Hatshepsut handed it down to her daughter Neferura.

The title *God's Wife of Amun* can be associated with the act of the god Amun ritually impregnating the king's mother to attest for his divine birth. Amun in the guise of the king (ritually the other way round!) had to enter the bedroom of the Queen and impregnate her in order to produce the next king.

Figure 17.
Musicians and dancers take part in a ritual ceremony at Karnak
The God's Wife took part in such ceremonies - at Karnak she is portrayed as burning images of Egypt's enemies and can be seen entering the sacred lake for purification before the ceremonies begin.

The *God's Wife of Amun* once conferred on the next heiress was the one whom the next king had to marry, which during this period was invariably a sister or half-sister.

When the *God's Wife* took part in temple ritual she was dressed in a short wig and a sheath dress tied at the waist:

1. The *God's Wife* was involved with the ritual of burning images of Egypt's enemies in a lighted brazier ie ritually destroying the names or images of enemies.

2. The next ritual in which the *God's Wife* was included involved an offering to the 17 gods at Karnak. The king and the accompanying priests performed the offering while the God's Wife looked on with her hands raised.

3. A third ritual follows where an entourage of King, priests and God's Wife carry out the 'Adoring the god for the Ennead and for the Kings of Upper and Lower Egypt and giving great praise by all the populace'.

4. Next they enter the Sacred Lake of the Temple to be purified.

5. Once purified they can then enter the inner sanctuary. This procession includes the King at the front followed by three priests and the God's Wife. The King then performs the rights before the statue of Amun-Ra. In the absence of the King this ritual would have been carried out by the priests. The God's Wife held property associated with this title and great authority in the cult of Amun-Ra.

Closely related to the title of God's Wife is the title 'God's Hand'. This refers to the hand that the creator god used to masturbate with in order to produce the first offspring, the god Shu and the goddess Tefnut.

Both of these titles, God's Wife and God's Hand have sexual connotations.

There has been some mystery concerning the exact nature of the ritual role played by the holder of the title God's Hand, but she was probably responsible for stimulating the god sexually to re-enact the original act of creation of the universe to prevent the world falling back into chaos.

The word for hand was feminine and this probably represented the female aspect of the creator god - his hand. Since the creator god came into being of himself and produced both a male and a female gods by self-procreation, then the creator god himself must have male and female attributes.

The God's Hand was therefore the female aspect of the god in the act of creation. In the temple ritual at Karnak, the King, the Good God, acted as the male essence of the creator god and was masturbated by the Queen, as the God's Hand, acting as the female aspect of the god.

In the Pyramid Texts the King is called the son of Atum 'of his body':

*'O Atum, raise this king up to you,
enclose him within your embrace,
for he is the son of your body for ever'
Pyramid Texts 213*

*'..Atum, father of the king, ascends to the sky.'
Pyramid Texts 992*

This enactment of the original act of creation, of the god Atum copulating with himself, within the walls of the Temple of Karnak had, therefore, another purpose - to bring forth, to bring into being the *next* king. This sexual act between the King and the God's wife not only ensured stability in the universe, life and order out of chaos, but also allowed the conception of the next god who was to be enthroned as king of Egypt.

'The King's mother (the Queen) was pregnant with him ... the King was fashioned by his father Atum.' Pyramid Texts 1466

If we imagine that once a year the King assumed his position as High Priest in temple ritual, as the male aspect of the creator god Atum, and his wife, the God's Wife, took on the role of the feminine aspect of the creator god, then they would both together perform the original act of creation where Atum copulated with himself. Other times this re-enactment of creation could have been carried out by the priests, perhaps using the statue of the ithyphallic Min.

It is difficult to imagine that the god's seed, ejaculated by the present king of Egypt, was allowed to simply 'fall to the ground'.

In the original act of creation Atum swallowed his own seed and then the fertile (feminine) part of his body, the womb, allowed this seed to germinate and grow.

One solution to this problem of the king's seed 'falling to ground' and one which would answer many questions concerning this act, namely that through oral sex the Queen, the God's Wife and feminine aspect of the kingly deity, swallowed the kings seed for its subsequent germination and birth of the next king.

Considering the Egyptian's knowledge of the workings of the female body, this is only natural.

A woman could be impregnated orally or via the vagina.

In the minds of the Egyptians these biological systems were connected. The woman's womb was simply providing the fertile environment for the seed to grow.

Further evidence comes from the accounts of the birth of the gods Shu and Tefnut in the Pyramid Texts, which describes their birth from the god Atum:

'O Atum-Kheperer, you became high on the height, you rose up as the benben stone in the Mansion of the Phoenix in On (Heliopolis), you spat out Shu, you expectorated Tefnut.' Pyramid Texts 1652-53

The god Atum gave birth to Shu and Tefnut through his mouth through which the seed had originally entered. In conclusion we may be reminded of the daily journey of the Sun-god through the body of the sky goddess Nut:

*Each evening Nut swallowed the sun,
during the night it travelled through her body (womb)
and she gave birth to it each morning.*

CPSIA information can be obtained at www.ICGtesting.com
Printed in the USA
LVIW01n1407230217
525230LV00014B/399